FORRI
THE BAKER

Edward Myers / *pictures by* **Alexi Natchev**

Dial Books for Young Readers New York

Published by Dial Books for Young Readers
A Division of Penguin Books USA Inc. / 375 Hudson Street / New York, New York 10014

Text copyright © 1995 by Edward Myers
Pictures copyright © 1995 by Alexi Natchev
All rights reserved / Designed by Nancy R. Leo
Printed in Mexico
First Edition
1 3 5 7 9 10 8 6 4 2

Library of Congress Cataloging in Publication Data
Myers, Edward.
Forri the baker / by Edward Myers ; pictures by Alexi Natchev.—1st ed.
p. cm.
Summary: When the Chlars invade the peaceful village of Ettai,
it is Forri the baker who comes up with an ingenious plan to save his fellow townspeople.
ISBN 0-8037-1396-7 (trade).—ISBN 0-8037-1397-5 (library)
[1. Bakers and bakeries—Fiction.   2. Bread—Fiction.]
I. Natchev, Alexi, ill.   II. Title.
PZ7.M98255Fo 1995   [E]—dc20   93-2468   CIP   AC

The full-color artwork was prepared using watercolors and colored pencils.
It was then scanner-separated and reproduced as red, blue, yellow, and black halftones.

To Joanne Greenberg E.M.

For Boiana A.N.

Many years ago there lived a baker in the village of Ettai. His name was Forri.

Forri was very thin. He dressed in baggy clothes sewn from old flour sacks, and he wore a shapeless white cloth cap that sagged over his head like a mass of unbaked dough.

Forri wasn't the only baker in town, but he was the best.
He made more kinds of bread than all the other bakers
combined. Not just round bread. Not just square bread. Not
just flat bread, tall bread, skinny bread. Forri made every
kind of bread—even kinds that no one in town had ever
seen, heard of, or eaten before. Root bread. Ice bread. Rose
bread. Nail bread.

At first the people of Ettai bought Forri's bread eagerly. After a while, though, some of them started to complain. "Pen bread, candle bread!" the villagers griped to one another. "Who cares if a loaf lights up your room? Who wants to *write* with bread?"

Rumors swelled like dough in a bread bowl. Forri was odd. Forri was strange. Forri was crazy. Villagers soon stopped buying from Forri, and the bakery failed. Forri moved to a shack at the edge of town.

Then the Chlars invaded Ettai.

The Chlars were the cruelest of all barbarians. Long ago, bands of them used to invade the mountain land, but none had raided Ettai for many years. Now, without warning,

dozens of Chlars simply showed up with their clubs, pikes, and battle-axes. No one in the village had a chance to resist. Besides, the people of Ettai were gentle by nature. The mountains had almost always kept out their enemies, so they knew little of fighting and possessed no weapons.

The Chlars shouted, "Back to your houses, all of you! Stay there until we tell you what to do!" Everyone obeyed. The Chlar army then withdrew, setting up several camps to surround the village. The warriors would return the next morning to take the people of Ettai prisoner and lead them away.

That night the villagers scurried through underground passageways and met in a cellar to plan their defense.

"What shall we do?" asked Ozzikki the blacksmith. "We can't just let these invaders conquer us."

"Bring your hammers and pokers," said Elara the weaver. "We'll drive back the Chlars."

Tikkaji the cobbler declared, "I'll bring my scrapers, gouges, and awls. Whatever we have we'll use to fight them."

Shouting and cheering, everyone agreed.

"Down with the Chlars!" they cried.

Then a voice at the back said, "That plan won't work."

All the men and women turned to see who spoke.

It was Forri the baker.

"There are too many Chlars," he said, "and they have too many weapons for us to fight them off. We'll never beat them with hoes, hammers, and awls."

"What do you suggest, then?" asked Ozzikki. "Wearing bread bowls for helmets? Using spoons for swords?"

Everyone laughed.

"No, something better."

Elara asked, "Better? Like what—maybe *bread*?"

People laughed and laughed.

"Of course," Forri told them. "What else but bread?"

The room fell silent. Forri was right about the Chlars having so many weapons, but what good was bread in fighting them?

"We'll hear what you have to say," Elara proclaimed. "If your plan isn't good, though, we'll go ahead with our own."

So they listened to him closely. Not many people felt convinced that Forri's idea would work. Still, no one could suggest anything better. The villagers decided to go along with Forri.

All night the men, women, and children of Ettai waited in their cottages. All night they watched, listened, and wondered when the invaders would enter the village again. All night they doubted that Forri the baker could save them from the Chlars.

The next morning, well before dawn, Forri passed out weapons to the villagers as they swarmed around him in the darkness. Swords, pikes, shields, bows, and arrows—Forri gave them to the men and women. Maces, spears, and lances too. All kinds of armor as well.

"Where did you find these weapons?" someone asked.

"I didn't find them," Forri told her. "Now take a sword from that pile. Time is short."

It was even shorter than they thought! For the stars had scarcely faded from the sky when almost a hundred Chlars showed up shouting, screaming, and shrieking with glee.

Then the Chlars stopped short.

The fading darkness revealed every wall, rooftop, tower, and balcony in town covered with men and women. And the half-light showed every person bristling with weapons.

Where had all the weapons come from? The invaders had searched every house, every shop, every granary and barn. Yet a whole forest of weapons had sprung up overnight! The Chlars saw the silhouette of this great army—the slant of the

pikes, the curve of the bows, the straightness of the arrows—
and they were afraid.

Little did they know it was only bread that frightened
them! Swords made of bread! Shields made of bread!
Helmets, breastplates, armor—all bread! Bows and arrows,
lances, axes! Maces! Pikes! Spears! Catapults! Everything was
bread! Nothing but bread!

The two forces faced each other for a long moment.

Then suddenly one of the Chlars shrieked an order.
The people of Ettai feared the worst.
With a great clatter of metal and wood and leather and stone, all the Chlars staggered back, turned, and fled. They ran out of town, up the valley, over the pass, and out of the mountain land.

The villagers stood there in silence. No one could believe what had happened.

Then, little by little, people started to talk—Elara the weaver, Ozzikki the blacksmith, Tikkaji the cobbler, and all the rest. Soon there was a great commotion of laughter, cheering, and shouts.

"Forri has saved us!"

"Long live Forri the baker!"

The villagers found Forri, lifted him to their shoulders, and carried him through the streets until they reached the town square. Then some people left, returning at once with butter, jelly, and jam.

And to celebrate their victory over the Chlars, everyone sat down together with Forri and ate all their weapons for breakfast.